W. E. Gladstone

An Academic Sketch

W. E. Gladstone

An Academic Sketch

ISBN/EAN: 9783337096199

Printed in Europe, USA, Canada, Australia, Japan

Cover: Foto ©Andreas Hilbeck / pixelio.de

More available books at **www.hansebooks.com**

THE ROMANES LECTURE

1892

An Academic Sketch

BY THE

RIGHT HON. W. E. GLADSTONE, M.P.

DELIVERED

IN THE SHELDONIAN THEATRE, OCT. 24, 1892

WITH ANNOTATIONS BY THE AUTHOR

𝔒𝔵𝔣𝔬𝔯𝔡

CLARENDON PRESS DEPOSITORY, 116 HIGH STREET

LONDON: HENRY FROWDE, AMEN CORNER, E.C.

1892

AN ACADEMIC SKETCH

————•————

BOTH after the extinction of the Roman Empire in the West, and during its senility, it may be affirmed, with some approach to historic truth, that there existed, throughout the range of the ancient civilisation, but one conspicuous instance of a standing attempt at systematic and orderly self-government, together with adjustment of disputes by the word rather than the sword. This example was to be found in the ordered fabric of the Christian Church; which, amidst surrounding decay, the living among the dead, steadily developed its organisation, and constructed its theology. Not that the action of its machinery, in its detail, was always prompt, regular, and certain. Efficiency such as that, in the moral sphere, is not given to man. But upon the whole, and by approximation, this mechanism did its work. A system was erected, alike vast and durable.

The resistance offered to this new agency was more tenacious and longer-lived[1] than some have supposed.

---

[1] See Beugnot, *Décadence du Paganisme dans l'Occident*, passim.

But it seems to have been more effective as a resistance offered by the party of privilege and possession, than in the intellectual domain. In general terms, and subject to partial qualification only, it may be affirmed that, amidst and around the vigorous Christian upgrowth, except in the region of military art, what we now denominate the lay mind seemed to sleep the sleep of death.

It was surely in accordance with all the laws of our nature that the new life, thus planted in its highest region by the Christian Faith, should in due time awaken its other agents from their lethargy. And the gradual extinction of Paganism, associated as it had been with intellect, and art, and every energy of worldly life, must have removed a formidable cause of jealousy.

Around the origins of the movement there might naturally gather, in an age that had but imperfect command either of communication, or of transmission, matter of a legendary character. We cannot, therefore, be greatly surprised at the beliefs long received that Charlemagne added to his other glories the honour of having founded the University of Paris, and that our own Alfred nursed the infancy of Oxford. These beliefs no longer subsist in any definite form. But Alcuin, English born and reared, and a zealous instructor of others in the learning he had himself acquired under Archbishop Egbert, was the intimate friend of Charlemagne, who made earnest though ineffectual efforts to fix permanently the sphere of his activity in Paris. In his teaching at his Abbey in Tours, as it is described by himself, he united the best elements accessible to him of divine and human knowledge, and thus served as a symbol of the true idea of a Christian University.

The troubled life of Alfred afforded less scope for the encouragement of learning: but there seems to have been space, in the mind of that truly glorious ruler, for every worthy object. The contention of Wood that he was the founder of Oxford has found zealous defenders abroad as well as at home. It is now abandoned. It appears indeed that, like Charlemagne, he was the founder[2] or patron of schools in various parts of England, which supplied in rudimental form something of what was reserved in its fulness for the future. But there is nothing to warrant our asserting either that the activity of Charlemagne took effect in Paris, or that of Alfred in Oxford.

It has been only in the present century, and, so far as our countrymen are concerned, only within its latter half, that the history of our national Universities has become the subject of the systematic study, which has produced, and is producing, such rich results, not least at this moment and in Oxford itself, through the comprehensive researches of Mr. Rashdall[3]. I dare not attempt even to touch the fringe of this great theme: but only to bring into view certain historic points which,

---

[2] Denifle, *Die Universitäten des Mittelalters bis 1400*, p. 240. Berlin, 1885.

[3] To whose courtesy I am indebted for the inspection of his learned and valuable proof-sheets, so far as they go, principally containing a luminous examination of the history of the University of Paris.

though they may be isolated, may be found not alto-
gether void either of interest or of freshness.

First, I would name that for which I have already
laid the ground. The Christian idea, taking possession
of man at the centre and summit of his being, could not
leave the rest of it a desert, but evidently contemplated
its perfection in all its parts. I appeal to those great and
comprehensive words of Saint Paul, which may have
been a prophecy not less than a precept, and which
enjoin us[4] to lay hold on 'whatsoever things are true,
whatsoever things are honest, whatsoever things are
just, whatsoever things are pure, whatsoever things are
lovely, whatsoever things are of good report.' It is
here conveyed to us that in the Christian religion there
lay, from the very first, the certain seed of all human
culture. But as, before the advent of that religion, the
great preparation of mankind to receive it was con-
ducted, within the boundaries of our civilisation, through
several races in their several seats, so, after it had come
into action, the entire scope of its office was not at once
made visible from any single point of view, any more
than the spectacle from Mount Pisgah[5] could command
all Palestine. Its work was developed in successive
efforts. The great spiritual power was the first to claim
possession of the field. In its own time, there sprang
up the grand and comprehensive conception of the
University.

But only by degrees. We learn that the name, now
stereotyped among us, had elder sisters. In particular

---

[4] Phil. iv. 8.   [5] Deut. xxxiv. 1.

there was the phrase *studium generale*. But this desig-
nation did not so much signify the extension of the
studies pursued, as the central and not merely local
character of the establishment[6]. So likewise we learn
that the early idea attached to the name *Universitas*
was not that of a high teaching institute. It meant an
union of persons for given purposes, and one regularly
organised; that is to say, a guild, or corporation.

So that, in its application to such an union, when
formed for the purpose of learning, its proper sense was
the combination into one regulated body of the teachers
and the scholars. Yet it always seems as if the word
University, soaring above the plane of antiquarian
learning, at the least prefigured for itself a very high
prerogative, and was fitted, and as it were predestined,
to convey the idea of its ultimate function, as the
treasure-house of all knowledge, and the *palæstra* of
universal instruction. This, be the name what it may,
was what the institution, from the days even of the
trivium and *quadrivium*, strove to be, and in a great
measure was.

As such it may be regarded variously from varying
points of view. Standing, in its origin, at the right hand
of the Christian Church, or on a parallel line with it, the
University seems to integrate the provision made for
the recovery and the training of our higher nature. As
regarded, however, from another point of view, it is not
only the complement, but also, in a more limited sense,
the rival, of the Church; the first great systematic effort

---

[6] Denifle, p. 12.

at what I have termed the lay mind to achieve self-assertion and emancipation.

We must not, however, overlook the fact that a large portion of the mediaeval Universities were founded under the authority of the Popes. This authority may have been given in discharge of the duty of the Church to cooperate in the promotion of culture. Or it may have been used as a defensive measure to keep in check the separate action of the lay element. It was also employed with great effect upon appeal, by interference in disputes, for the aggrandisement of the central power. And we must remember that neither the papal nor the regal authority called into existence the oldest Universities. Salerno and Bologna were possibly due to professional exigencies. And about ten Universities, several of them with provision for teaching in all the faculties, appear to have been at work before Papal action began. They were in the main voluntary foundations. But, in the year 1222, Frederic the Second made a beginning, on the part of the State, by founding the University of Naples.

The grand scene of conflict between the Court of Rome and local autonomy was, as might be expected, in Paris. But the Universities supplied a battle-ground, on which all the living energies of the time were in constant struggle. Not only the great central Church power as against local forces, but sovereign and subject, seculars and regulars, schools of philosophy, careers of education, the municipal and the academic forces, continually rocked the cradles of these great institutions; and the fact of so much growth amidst so much contention shows with how vigorous a life the body politic was endowed. But the one great standing competition was that of the ecclesiastical element with the lay. It is traceable alike in the broader and in the minor channels [7].

It does not follow from what has been said that, in any normal or healthy state of things, the University and the Church are adversaries: or even are antagonists in any other sense than as two rowers, one on the right, and the other on the left, portions of whose force neutralise one another, unite nevertheless to propel the boat.

This dualism, this competition of the lay and the ecclesiastical forces, is visible by the side of their co-operation, all along the stream of history. Was it the first presage of this relation between University and Church, when Saint Francis exhibited his apprehension of the great academic power, then in its mere infancy, by his indisposition to see the members of his order incorporated in Universities? And, if so, was it a curious retribution following upon that reluctance, when the strong stream of fact so peremptorily overruled the will of the Founder, that, during the thirteenth

---

[7] In 1312 Pope Clement V gave his sanction to the original University of Dublin on the petition of the Archbishop. But this harmony did not exclude jealousy; for in the first Statutes it was provided that the Chancellor should receive institution from the Diocesan, and, invested as he was with the spiritual jurisdiction, should also take an oath of obedience. This University was at work in 1320; but it appears soon to have fallen into decay, extinction, and oblivion. See Denifle, pp. 639-42.

and fourteenth centuries, the Franciscan Order gave to Oxford the larger number of those remarkable, and even epoch-making men, who secured for this University such a career of glory in mediaeval times?

I note then, in the first place, as marking the normal relation, in a Christian land, between the University and the Church, this distinctness of colour, this competition, and this yet more prevailing cooperation.

The particular terms of the relation could not, indeed, permanently continue without change. The seas had been little traversed, the surface of the earth but partially explored: the field of human experience had to be immeasurably widened and diversified, the relation between man and man to be fundamentally altered in respect of knowledge, of subjection, and of intercourse. The art of criticism, arbitrary and rash, yet indispensable and invaluable, had to emerge as almost a new creation of the human mind.. The very foundations for the investigation of Nature, in her vast and varied realms, were yet to be laid, or laid anew. Wealth, too, with all its subtle influences, was to be increased, and probably has yet to be increased beyond all older conception and belief. Though divine knowledge might also in various ways advance and be enlarged, it was hardly possible that progress in this region could present any analogous magnitude of scale, or of results. On the whole, it could not but be that the world-power should gain largely in force upon the Church-power: and of the world-power, in its least grovelling and most upward aspects, the University was the proper representative upon the field of human culture.

On the climax of this change I may presently have to say a word. For the present, I have only to observe that, according to the principle of old English law, the University, as such, is a lay, and not an ecclesiastical foundation; and that this principle is a deep principle, and is also a just principle.

We have before us, at the point we have now reached, the idea of the University full-formed, to harbour, cherish, and develop all the knowledge, suitable for training, which the rolling years might add to the human store: both its traditions, and its acquisitions; or, in the words of Euripides—

πατρίους παραδοχάς, ἅς θ' ὁμήλικας χρόνῳ
κεκτήμεθ' [8].

In the chart of that knowledge, theology had not a chronological precedence, except as we may presume it in cases where the *nucleus* of the University lay in Schools attached to ecclesiastical foundations. Speaking generally, the foundation, according to the old formula, was in Arts. The *trivium* and *quadrivium* were not tied down to the limitations of their first intention in their several items, but with a more generous and expansive meaning were in possession of the ground [9]: but theology soon obtained its place, and asserted something of a maternal sway.

Let us now proceed to inquire what share, in point of date and amount, fell to England, in the practical

---

[8] Bacchae, 201 (Elmsley).
[9] De Ménerval, *Paris*, vol. i. p. 279.

application of the great idea, during the first and not least brilliant period of academic history.

It is to Italy, richer as she was than any other country in the remains of the ancient civilisation, thàt we must accord the honour of having owned the earliest establishments to which the name of University has been accorded [10]. Salerno is the oldest among them; drawing doubtfully its title from the ninth century, and famous only as a medical school. Bologna follows in the twelfth century, and is joined with Paris by Denifle, partly on the ground of a priority enjoyed by both, Bologna perhaps having slightly the advantage, and partly because these exhibited the two forms of foun-dation which had most to do with supplying patterns for later establishments. Bologna [11], however, earned its early fame only as the grand school of law: in which capacity it attracted students largely from beyond the Alps; while in the course of time other studies were gradually grouped around it without at first forming part of the University.

One, and only one, other University commenced its career in the twelfth century. It was then that Oxford became definitely entitled to the name, with an equip-ment in all the faculties.

Cambridge dated somewhat later; for it is first in the year 1209 that a trustworthy notice of it is found [12]. Like Oxford, it was supplied with the four faculties. And, like Oxford, as well as Paris and Bologna, it owed

---

[10] Denifle, p. 307.   [11] *Ibid.* pp. 40 *seqq.*

[12] *Ibid.* p. 369.

its existence to no exercise of authority either by the State or by the Church, but to that free and spontaneous impulse, which some of the most learned inquirers into academic origins regard as the noblest feature of their early history.

At a later date, in the year 1318, and at the request of King Edward II, Pope John XXII issued for Cambridge what purported to be a document of foundation. But the institution had been long at work, and it may probably then have been suffering from temporary difficulty or decline. At one time, in 1229, she gave shelter to a body of students from Paris. At another, in 1240, she performed the same hospitable office for Oxford. For the vicissitudes of academic existence were at that time no less rude and chequered than that existence itself was masculine and intense, and from time to time compelled a resort to such shelter in several quarters. But Cambridge did not attain the fulness of her stature until a much later date.

It is Paris which among the Mediaeval Universities, say, from the twelfth until the fourteenth century, towers above all the rest as the mart of teaching and of learning, but especially of theological learning. She drew men, as other great markets draw, along the converging lines gradually formed by mental as well as by material traffic. Paris had that *potior principalitas*, which, in the earliest Christian ages, so largely brought about a confluence of ecclesiastical causes towards Rome. She had much of that command from circumstances and situation which now makes London the money-market of the world at large. Youth flocked thither in crowds to learn. But on a still wider, and indeed an astonishing scale, did all distinguished teachers repair thither to teach. From the careful work of Dr. Budzinsky [13] it would seem as though a large majority of the more learned men from all the European countries gravitated to Paris, both for study and for the instruction of others, at some period, and often for a large portion, of their lives. It serves, I think, to enhance our idea of the noble enthusiasm for learning that then prevailed, when we thus see that men would not be bound by local circumscriptions, or rest satisfied with anything less than the best and highest of what their world could supply. Again, in its influence as a model, and in its historical greatness as a national and even an international power, none can contest the primacy of Paris. But while thus endeavouring to do justice to the wonderful University of that wonderful city, I believe there is still something to be said which may well satisfy every child of Oxford with regard to the position which then fell to her lot.

We cannot indeed trace so well, as in the case of Paris, her preparation for full academic life by a long experience of teaching institutes less fully organised, and combined by no common link. Some presumption to this effect seems to arise from the rapidity with which the University, when formed, came to tread in the footmarks of her elder, yet scarcely elder,

---

[13] *Die Universität Paris, und die Fremden an derselben im Mittelalter.* Von Dr. Alexander Budzinsky. Berlin, 1876.

sister. Under King Stephen, and before the twelfth century had well run half its course, the connection of Oxford with the names of Vacarius and Pullus [14] appears to show that the place was then a more or less active seat of learning. Apart from this, Oxford is mentioned as already an University with a Chancellor in the year 1201 [15]. But considerably earlier, in 1189, Giraldus Cambrensis had read there his *Topographia Cambriæ*, and had on a set day held a reception for the doctors of the several faculties. According to Roger Wendover, there were in 1209 [16], when the great dispersion took place, about 3000 students in Oxford, or nearly thrice the numbers of 1830, and the estimate is deemed by Denifle not to betray large exaggeration. From this date we may pass onwards to 1252 [17], when the Chronicles record this most striking testimony: *Oxonialis Universitas, æmula Parisiensis.*

Æmula Parisiensis: not probably in the number of its students, though the estimate at this time boldly mounts to 15,000; not in the attractive force which drew to it nearly all famous teachers; not in other points, at which I have slightly glanced; but in one vital particular it may seem that, so far as I can learn, and as

---

[14] Denifle, p. 247.

[15] I have relied here on the acceptance of the statement by Denifle, p. 244. But the document on which it rests is a forgery according to Lyte's *History of Oxford*, p. 243. Lyte, however, supplies evidence at p. 14 of his History on the 'populousness' of the schools of Oxford in the end of the twelfth century. He also substitutes the *Topographia Hibernica* for the *Cambrensis* (p. 13).

[16] Denifle, p. 242.　　　　　　　　[17] *Ibid.* p. 252.

has before me once or twice been intimated[18], Oxford may deliver a challenge even to Paris, and not fear defeat. That is, in the number of great scholars and great men whom at this early period of her own existence she drew forth into intellectual life, and reared as in a seed-bed.

It is further singular that the time, when she burst into this extraordinary richness of bloom, should have been also the time when the two mendicant orders of Dominicans and Franciscans acquired a dominant influence in the University. For it appears that, about 1250, the exercises of bachelors for degrees were read by custom in the house of the one order or the other. And Grostête, though not a Franciscan, lectured in the Franciscan convent. Lastly, we may observe that the greatest names belonging to Oxford, in the thirteenth and fourteenth centuries, are not of the order of Saint Dominic, to whom Dante awards the intellectual brightness of the cherub[19], but in the ranks of the seraphic Francis, who could not abide the world even in its academic form. These men were men of English birth. But the fame of their school was such that Franciscans flocked to it, not only from Scotland and Ireland, but from France, Italy, Spain, Portugal, and Germany.

The most famous among these luminaries of Oxford

---

[18] See something of an intimation to this effect in Hallam, *Literature of Europe*, vol. i. p. 16; who appears to rely on Wood, vol. i. p. 159.

[19] *Paradiso*, c. xi. 39-41.

were probably Alexander of Hales, Adam Marsh, one of his most distinguished pupils, and the close friend of Grostête; Archbishop Peckham, an experienced mathematician, Duns Scotus, William of Ockham [20], the celebrated nominalist, and lastly, the greatest probably of them all, Roger Bacon, perhaps the most striking British intellect of the middle ages; who spent many of his years in prison, and of whom some skilled students in philosophy and history have not shrunk, in our own time, from declaring that in originality and power he must be held to excel his illustrious namesake, the famous Francis, Lord Bacon [21].

The renown and greatness of these Oxford Franciscans may perhaps best, as well as most briefly, be estimated from the number of cases in which they acquired that superlative distinction of mediaeval learning, the appropriation of a special, characteristic, and laudatory epithet to their names. They figure largely on the Oxford list which I have brought together— Alexander of Hales was *Doctor irrefragabilis*. Duns Scotus was *Doctor subtilis*. William of Ware was *Doctor fundatus*. John of Baconthorpe was *Doctor resolutus*. Richard of Middleton was *Doctor solidus*. Burley was *Doctor simplex*. Bradwardine was *Doctor profundus*. Roger Bacon was *Doctor mirabilis*.

---

[20] His belonging to Oxford has been contested, but in the present state of the controversy I have thought it my safest course to adhere to the common tradition.

[21] I refer to Sir John Herschel and Mr. Lewes, as having, I believe, formed this estimate.

William of Ockham was *Doctor invincibilis et singu-laris*[22]. These epithets are, I believe, coin of European rather than of purely British currency.

The names all belong to Oxford, and to the thir-teenth and fourteenth centuries. The great men of the Franciscan Order, whom I first enumerated, are matched, I believe, only by a few beyond it: by Grostête, Bishop of Lincoln, whom Gower calls the 'great clerk'; by Archbishop Bradwardine, and Wiclif. Bradwardine is commemorated in a couplet of Dryden, founded upon Chaucer, which runs:

> I cannot bolt this matter to the bran,
> As Bradwardine and holy Austin can[23].

To Wiclif I shall again refer. But I think enough has now been said to afford some colour of justification for the attempt to match Oxford in this one respect with Paris: where William of Champeaux, with his rebellious but transcendent pupil Abelard, rather ushered in the University proper, than belonged to it. I do not know whether a list of those whom in the strict sense she reared, and who attained to high excellence, is accessible. One very great name was contributed to it by England, for Stephen Langton was her *alumnus*. I have spoken of matching Oxford with Paris: but in the present state of the evidence, and within the limit I

---

[22] These particulars are given in the British Section of the work of Dr. Budzinsky under the respective names: or in Mr. Lyte's *History of the University of Oxford*, p. 156.

[23] Dryden's *Fables*, Tale of the Nun's Priest.

have described, it seems as if we might claim for her the palm.

We have now passed through the period, which, unless, in that here as well as elsewhere, the victory of philosophy was the death of classicism, we may term the golden age of Oxford. After say 1400, we pass at once into a darker period:

> But yet we know,
> Where'er we go,
> That there hath passed away a glory from the earth [24].

Indeed there is no subsequent time at which we can with historic fidelity claim on her behalf a position so commanding. The decay extended to both our Universities. The causes may be variously regarded. Collier [25] refers it mainly to the absorption of Church benefices by the monasteries. It seems more than probable that the wars of the fifteenth century, which had the double vice of being intestine and of being dynastic, had much to do with it. A third efficient cause is well suggested by Mr. Lyte, in the stringent measures of Archbishop Arundel against Lollardism, which greatly limited the freedom of thought that had been possessed and used by Ockham and his predecessors.

It is pleasant, however, to refer not only to the presence and activity of Erasmus in both our Universities, before and after A. D. 1500, but to the glowing eulogy which he passed upon their college life. Down

---

[24] Wordsworth's Ode on Intimations of Immortality.
[25] *Eccl. History*, vol. iii. p. 399.

to this period, and in the reflected light of the Renas-
cence [26], Oxford had retained her relative superiority
over Cambridge; which has no group of names to
compete with those of Selling, Linacre, Grocyn, Colet,
and Sir Thomas More. It may also be observed
that, in the year 1476 [27], Oxford had obtained her
printing-press; but Cambridge was possessed of no
such instrument when Erasmus quitted it in 1514.

We now pass into the sixteenth century; the age of
specifically national development, and one singularly
prolific, as I conceive, of powerful minds and characters.
But it was not great as an academic age, while the
relative positions of the two Universities also under-
went a total change. To her manifest and indeed
hardly measureable superiority in the earlier centuries,
Oxford had now bidden a long farewell.

It was indeed a century too polemical to be favourable
to the development of a vigorous academic life. An in-
teresting Table, with which Mr. Mullinger has supplied
us in his recent sketch of the history of Cambridge,
shows that, between 1500 and 1560, the Baccalau-
reate [28] was only given to a number averaging annually
less than 50. This decline impartially includes the
religious extremes of Mary and of Edward VI. With
the reign of Elizabeth an improvement began; but it is
also true that, from the date of her accession, the theo-

---

[26] I have ventured upon following several writers of credit in
the employment of this word in preference to borrowing *Renais-
sance*, which has no advantage over it, from the French.

[27] See Ames's *History of Printing*.

[28] Which she now confers upon some 700 persons annually.

logical atmosphere had somewhat cooled. It seems, however, that other and not unimportant influences helped to lower the academic pulse. Ascham says that among the prevailing evils there was none more grave than the large admission of the sons of rich men, indifferent to solid and far-reaching study[29]: while Bucer recorded his opinion that the indolent fellows[30] who were growing old on the different collegiate foun- dations, were an *incubus* on the University. Such academic activity as still remained was in Cambridge rather, than in Oxford, as is shown by the names of Ascham, Cheke, Thomas Smith, and the illustrious Cecil, who was for a short time a Lecturer in Greek.

It was, however, into polemical channels that the principal energies of the Universities, in the sixteenth century, were drawn. In the University of Cambridge, as it is contended, the Reformation in England had its real commencement[31]. And most certainly Oxford, though she reared Hooper[32], the stiffest of all Puritans, has no claim to this distinction. On the other hand it may, I think, be said that the greatest English move- ment of that century, which engraved so deep a mark on history, had its first foundations laid far more in nationalism than in theology. But, together with the

---

[29] Mullinger, History of Cambridge, p. 88.

[30] *Ibid.* p. 104.

[31] Mullinger, Preface.

[32] Tyndale, to whom I believe we are much indebted for his labours in the translation of the Holy Scriptures, was bred in Oxford, but on turning towards Lutheranism, found it too hot to hold him.—Wood's *Ath.*, vol. i. col. 94.

great national movement under Henry VIII, vivid, though to a great extent latent, religious influences were at work ; and of these influences on the reforming side, not the greater part only, but almost the whole belong to Cambridge. Except the influences of Jewell, and of Nowell, Oxford did not, I believe, contribute a single name that can be quoted to the promotion of the move-ment. The three famous prelates, who have been monumentally commemorated in Oxford for reasons other than academic, were Cambridge men. The Elizabethan Bishops, generally, were Cambridge men. A student of Cambridge denounced the indulgences of Leo X in 1517, the same year with Luther. Bilney, another genuine Reformer; and Tyndale, whom we gratefully remember for his labours in the formation of the English Bible, found refuge in Cambridge, at least for a period, when driven from Oxford. Every Archbishop of Canterbury, between Warham and Abbot, excepting Pole, was a Cambridge man.

But we are not to suppose that Edwardian or Eliza-bethan bishops occupied the same hegemonic position with regard to the religious movement in England, as was held by Luther and Melanchthon, by Calvin and Zwinglius, and even by others, second to these in fame, on the continent of Europe. From whatever cause, possibly from the strong infusion of political and secular ingredients, the religious movement of England was, in the dominant circles, comparatively a feeble one. We may take, as specimens of the laity, Cromwell and Somerset; strong men, but men to whose strength little was contributed by religion. Within the ecclesiastical circles, the proof of this relative weakness is supplied by the single fact that to reform our service-books, and to instruct our candidates for holy orders, we were driven to invoke the aid of foreigners. Bucer, wisest of them all, filled the Divinity Chair at Cambridge, and when he died Musculus, another foreigner, was recommended for it; Peter Martyr was Regius Professor in Oxford; Alasco, Fagius, and Ochino are well-known names of men who exercised in the Edwardian period their powerful influence upon ecclesiastical affairs, in aid of the national deficiencies.

The large relative share of Cambridge at this critical period was enhanced by the fact that there was a difference in the prevalent theological cast of the two Universities. Oxford was on the losing side; and perhaps the very ablest men among those she reared, such as Allen, Campion, Stapleton, and the rest, were ejected and suppressed. It might be said, without any gross perversion of historical truth, that in the sixteenth century the deepest and most vital religious influences within the two Universities respectively were addressed, at Oxford to the making of recusants, at Cambridge to the production of Zwinglians and Calvinists. Undoubtedly it was Cambridge that reared the various forms of Puritanism, which seems to have divided with Recusancy the warmer religious life of those days. She produced Whitaker, the champion of the more temperate Puritanism: she also produced Browne, the leader of the consistent and thorough-going Brownists. She claims likewise Travers and Cartwright, who stand between the two: and it is further characteristic of the

relative attitude of the Universities that, against Cartwright, there rose up from Oxford Richard Hooker,
the first really great name in English theology since
the Reformation, who has received the glowing eulogy
of Mr. Hallam [33], and who remains a classic of British
literature, while his opponent, I fear, has been given
to the cobweb and the moth.

Through the first half of the seventeenth century,
the strife of Anglican and Puritan raged fiercely in the
womb of the Church of England ; but the Universities,
considered as academic bodies, were in fairer condition
than under the fiercer strain and stress of the Reformation.   The period which followed the Restoration
was perhaps the best they had known since the days of
Erasmus.   Then came into being, through the agency
of Oxford, the Royal Society for the promotion of
Natural Science : and then, with rival honour, grew in
Cambridge a school of Philosophy which is adorned by
the names of Whichcote, Cudworth, John Smith, and
Henry More.

But there is another growth, mainly of the seventeenth century, which has sufficient greatness to
demand notice on academic grounds, although it
belongs strictly to the sphere of the Church. That is,
the formation of what might be termed, or might safely
have been termed, until a very recent day, the standard

---

[33] *Constitutional History*, vol. i. 230 *seqq.* (4to edition).   I am
informed by Lord Acton that Hooker received an eulogy yet
more remarkable from Dr. Döllinger, in the earlier period of his
long life, and in his Lectures on dogmatic theology, *Locus de
Ecclesiâ.*

theology of the English Church: that theology into which, by a normal process, it settled down, when the tempest of sheer violence had been sufficiently allayed to give fair scope and shelter for the action of tranquil thought and the labours of the pen. It attracted the sympathies of great foreigners, such as Casaubon, Grotius, and De Dominis [34]; and it was marked, from the time of Andrewes onwards, by deep learning and by great and varied ability. The Bishops of the Restoration, if judged by results, were no small ecclesiastical statesmen. The men who executed the Authorised Translation of the Scriptures were not mere pedants, fanatics, or bookworms. The Anglican divines of the seventeenth century were, probably to a man, reared within the Universities. It appears to me that of the work which they jointly performed, though this is not perhaps the general impression, the larger and weightier part was due to Cambridge.

If now we proceed to take the seventeenth and eighteenth centuries in one group, and endeavour to test the relative greatness of the two Universities, during that period, by the greatness of the individual

---

[34] Every one is aware that De Dominis returned to Italy, and it is, I believe, certain that in some terms and in some sense he renounced his own previous action with respect to the Church of England. But he was treated by the Latin Church, after his death, as a heretic; and it may be a question whether he did not act all along upon that view of the Church at large which was resolutely held in the seventeenth century by Bishop Goodman of Gloucester, and perhaps (within my own memory) by that devout, eloquent, and attractive clergyman of the present century, Mr. R. Waldo Sibthorp.

men whom they produced, Cambridge confronts her
ancient rival with that formidable triad, which I know
not how we are to match. The names of Bacon,
Milton, and Newton, which I arrange in the order of
chronology rather than that of greatness, are names
before which we can only bow.

In naming Milton, I am led to observe by the way
upon a fact which may or may not be worth examination
as to its cause. It is that, until the close of the last
century, Oxford had made hardly an appreciable con-
tribution, so far as I am aware, to the noble catalogue
of English Poets. During the nineteenth century,
which is almost entirely excluded from the scope of
this address, she has shown no such deficiency. She
can claim, from Shelley onwards, many real poets,
and some who have a title to greatness. This very
fact gives point to the question why or how it is that
there should have been for many generations almost
a void in this department of her academic history. I
now revert to the main stream of my remarks.

With reference to one of the three superlative names,
lately credited to Cambridge, there may be those who
would contend that philosophers are largely to be
judged by the influence they exercise; and that the
thoughts of Locke operated far more powerfully, in the
generations which followed him, than those of Bacon.
And this I suppose to be emphatically true.

As the German philosophy has in recent times largely
dominated the thought of the world, it is matter of
interest for us all to look back to its fountain-heads. In
a work of authority by Zart, on the amount of influence

brought to bear on that philosophy, for the eighteenth century, by English writers from Bacon onwards, that influence is stated to have largely exceeded any that was drawn from other foreign sources. Further, we learn that the power exercised by Locke, and familiarly known to have been extensive in France, went far beyond that of any other British writer, and indeed reached such a height in Germany also, and in America, as well as in England, that it can only be compared with the dominion of Aristotle over the Middle Age, or that of Kant over the German writers of the present century[35].

Locke was favoured by the tide which runs in the affairs of men. However utilitarian may be the tendency imputed to the Baconian philosophy, the writings of Locke bore more sensibly than those of Bacon upon palpable interests, and current questions; and they were more eminently in accordance with the ruling, or rising, tendencies of his time. So his thoughts wrought upon the thought of man at large with an energy enhanced by the leverage thus given them. But if we grant that Locke, in this way, may have been lifted above his proper level, it remains as a real curiosity in literary history, after allowing for every political prejudice, that we should find a man of the calibre of Hume describing his works (with those of some others) as compositions

---

[35] See *Einfluss der englischen Philosophie seit Bacon auf die deutsche Philosophie des 18. Jahrhunderts.* Von G. Zart. Berlin, 1881.

'the most despicable both for style and matter,' for which the Whig predominance of the eighteenth century had obtained in England an undue cele-brity[36].

That eighteenth century does not offer us a brilliant period for either University. The old superstition of passive obedience and non-resistance, which had been a parasitic growth out of the peculiar incidents of the English Reformation, had speedily lost, after the Revolution, whatever it might theretofore have pos-sessed of consistency or dignity. But it survived that epoch in both Universities[37], and with a conspicuous obstinacy of life in Oxford; which had the question-able distinction of being, long afterwards, the theatre of the latest disturbance of public order ever effected in the name and by the partisans of the Stuarts. This longevity of a peculiar and quite superannuated opinion may have been due in part to the innate conservatism then sheltered in all the nooks and crannies of our ecclesiastical organisation, and in part to that determined tenacity of the English character, which is so beneficial and noble in a good cause, so dangerous in a bad one.

---

[36] Hume's *History of England*, vol. ix. p. 524, text and footnote. Chap. lxxi.

[37] The Oxford Address of 1683 to Charles II has commonly been gibbeted alone. But the Cambridge Address of the same year is fully worthy, in point of principle, though not of length, to keep company with it. Both may be seen sufficiently in Collier's *Eccl. Hist.* vol. viii. 490-6. Such documents could not appear after 1688-9; but the sentiment which prompted them long survived their production.

The Universities were not now, as in the Middle Age, the home of all the culture that the time could boast. Medicine drew off to the great towns[38]; law found its home in the Inns of Court. The clerical element completely dominated both Oxford and Cambridge. But, while relatively strong, it was intrinsically, that is academically, weak. Lord Stanhope[39] has explained, I think with much felicity, one and perhaps the main cause of decadence of the clergy. They were entirely out of sympathy with the Hanoverian dynasty; and they could not be transformed into loyal subjects by force. The course pursued was to select Bishops with a regard to their political conformity, and to plant them among a clergy whom, except occasionally, they appear to have simply let alone. No attempt was made either to supply deficiencies, or to furnish a remedy for abuses. Privilege remained intact; for none would invade the hornets' nest. Indolence and greed had their unrestricted reign.

Huber, to whom we owe gratitude for the first attempt at a living reproduction of our academic life, and whose research gravitated, throughout his work, by preference towards Oxford, puts the Universities of the last century upon their trial, and finds for them a sort of acquittal. The substance of his contention is that, while they were far indeed from corresponding with any comprehensive or normal conception, they

---

[38] It may, however, be noticed that Dr. Freind and Dr. Meade, the two leading London practitioners of the era of Geo. I, were both educated at Oxford.

[39] Stanhope, *History of England*, ii. 370.

were in harmony with the actual standards of the nation of the time. And he holds that, if a particular organ of the national life were in default, and there is no censure, or attempt at amendment from without, we must, in justice, refer the blame not to the particular organ as such, but to the condition of the national life taken at large [40].

The well-known pair of admirable epigrams, by Dr. Trapp and Sir William Browne [41] respectively, which belong to the reign of George I, give not a fair, but not a wholly unfair, representation of the comparative position of the two Universities, in relation to the new political settlement, and the accompanying direction of the public mind. I had not intended to recite the text of these epigrams, as they may be so familiar to a large portion of this audience as to render such a recital commonplace. But as I gather that they are not well known to a portion, even if only a minority of those whom I have the honour to address, I will give the lines, and also the occasion which drew them forth.

It appears that King George I sent, at about the same time, a troop of cavalry to Oxford, and a gift of books to Cambridge University. Hereupon Dr. Trapp produced his capital epigram—

'The King, regarding with impartial eyes
The wants of both his Universities,

---

[40] Huber, *Die englischen Universitäten*, vol. ii. p. 430.

[41] Founder of the prize for epigrams: perhaps with some retrospect on his own performance.

> To Oxford sent a troop of horse ; and why ?
> That learned body wanted loyalty.
> To Cambridge books he sent, as well discerning
> That that right loyal body wanted learning.

He was met by the even better epigram of Sir William Browne, in reply on behalf of Cambridge—

> The king to Oxford sent a troop of horse,
> For Tories own no argument but force :
> With equal sense to Cambridge books he sent,
> For Whigs admit no force but argument.

We may safely affirm that the outer world was less scantily represented by the Cambridge than by the Oxford of the day; and Cambridge also, for the time, had the larger share in supplying the country with its most eminent statesmen. Yet it is less true to say that she was Whig while Oxford was Tory, than that she was Tory while Oxford was Jacobite. For we learn that, when the strength of parties was tested, the Cambridge Tories used to beat the Whigs by at least two to one [42]. We may grant however to our favoured sister that this Toryism, if it did not represent chivalry, represented progress.

Yet it may be contended that Cambridge cannot for this period produce a list of academic figures equal to those by which Oxford was honoured even in the midst of prevailing decay. The weighty names of Blackstone and of Sydenham show that some shadow at least of the oldest Faculties still rested on her. But to these we join Wesley and Johnson, Gibbon and Adam Smith, Berkeley [43] and Butler.

---

[42] Monk's *Life of Bentley* (4to), p. 294. [43] See Note I at end.

Five of these six great men, it may probably be said with truth, have received, and are receiving still, their due. But can this be affirmed of the last, who is, however, estimated by some as the greatest of them all? The case of Butler is indeed peculiar. He has not, like some other authors, been borne down by bulk: his whole works hardly exceed the dimensions of a three-volume novel. His 'noble intellect' is frankly commended by one of our sceptical writers [44], who evidently accords to him the old funereal eulogy *si Pergama dextrâ Defendi possent.* His strong hand for years together held James Mill on the brink of the atheism, into which he eventually fell. He, who is among the most circumspect of philosophers, has asserted, by a kind of prophetic anticipation, some of the most daring *dicta* of modern science and theology. Yet not even a single morsel of his writings has ever been translated into a single foreign tongue [45]. And in the really important treatise of Zart, to which reference has already been made, we have a list of no fewer than forty-eight British writers, in connection with the influence they had exercised on German philosophy in its plastic stage: but among those forty-eight the name of Butler is not found. And yet where is the writer who has entered so profoundly, and with such measured strength, into the constitutive or governing laws applicable to moral conduct, that is to say for the whole rational life of man; or who has laid

---

[44] Miss Hennell, *On the Sceptical Tendency of Butler's ' Analogy.'*

[45] This assertion requires correction: see Note II at end.

so firmly and so scientifically, from a Christian point of departure, the foundations of the relation between the seen world and its unseen Ruler?

Surely this great man may be counted now, as Keats was counted when Shelley wrote the *Adonais,* among

Th' inheritors of unfulfilled renown.

So then, with others of the band of the Immortals, he abides his time. And I believe it will reckon as not the least among the glories of Oxford, if she can show, when called to account, that in the exercise of her teaching office she has done constant justice to her illustrious child, and to her own traditions, and to the exigencies of the future, in connection with him.

Let me now endeavour briefly to present the dis-tinctive character of our two Universities to view with reference to one other particular. That particular is the different proportions in which they may have divided their energies between the production of men of thought on the one hand, or men of action on the other. For, there may be a difference in the comparative adaptation of their respective methods and institutions, and of their interior and essential genius, to the one or the other purpose.

It is not, I think, very difficult to point out, in the region of action as distinguished from the world of thought, the greatest ecclesiastics of the English Church since the Conquest. I suppose them to be Becket; Langton, who led the Barons in extorting *Magna Charta* from King John, and who acted no less stoutly against the great Pope Innocent III, his patron;

Wolsey, intercepted in his great career by his yet more masterful sovereign; Laud, who stands upon the historic stage halfway between culprit and martyr; and finally John Wesley, whose single will, energy of character, and devotion, rather than power purely intellectual, are now after a century and a half represented in the English-speaking race by organised bodies with adherents estimated, I believe, by none at less than twelve millions in number, and by some at a much higher figure.

There are others, such as Grostête, and Gardiner in his later period: great names in history, but hardly competing with those previously produced. Again, there are men who have played conspicuous and weighty parts, such as Cranmer: a prelate of vigorous and comprehensive talents, but one who, in a great post and period (and always excepting the last, and more than heroic scene), seems in action mainly to represent minds other than his own. Again, there was Simeon, who was contented, through his long life, with the *fallentis semita vitæ* in a Fellowship at King's, yet who deserves a place, and a very honourable place, in the history of both Church and University. But there are two, who perhaps ought to stand even on the same level with the five great names I have selected, making seven in all; subject however to this qualification, that they were not statesmen of the Church, or men in whom action eclipsed or overshadowed thought, but were thinkers whose written word passed, indeed, into action as wine into the blood, but mediately, through the minds and in the deeds of others, rather than their own.

The first of these is Wiclif, whose singular destiny it was to produce in Bohemia results far wider, and far more potent, than in his own sphere and country. The second is a name which may still touch living memories. It is Newman: who principally, and in half a lifetime, set a mark upon the mind and inner spirit of the English Church, which it is likely to carry through many generations.

Of these seven men, Becket is antecedent to University History, and was educated at Merton on the Wandle, with which, however, the earliest of Oxford colleges had a traditional connection. Langton was probably born about the middle of the twelfth century; and if so, his youthful training fell upon the period, seemingly a very short period, when Paris was in full work as an University, and Oxford had not yet regularly begun. The other five names on this distinguished roll—Wiclif, Wolsey, Laud, Wesley, Newman, —are one and all not only found in the Oxford lists, but also intimately associated by residence, and by personal action and interest, with the history, and indeed with the very soul, of this University.

My selection of names, whether accurate or not, is intended to invite an impartial estimate of the character so chosen, according to power and to results, rather than according to any award of praise or blame, or any special distribution of our personal antipathies or sympathies. There is however one among them whose title to his place may not be readily accorded. The name of Laud has now for two centuries and a half been largely visited with disapproval, sometimes with

contempt.   So great a writer as Lord Macaulay [46] finds
in Strafford a character of 'great abilities, eloquence,
and courage,' but in Laud only a man of 'narrow under-
standing,' of a 'nature rash and irritable,' and of small
'commerce with the world.'   Yet these two men were
the Pylades and Orestes of civil life; there seems to
have been established a thorough community of soul
between them; and it might be hard to show any
single point of action or opinion on which they dif-
fered.   For the political sentiments and judicial acts
of either I have not a word to say except that they
were expiated by both upon the scaffold, and that
they in no way enter into the ground of the present
estimate.   Of Laud as a Churchman it ought to have
been remembered, at least in extenuation, that he was
the first Primate of all England for many generations
who proved himself by his acts to be a tolerant theo-
logian.   He was the patron not only of the saintly and
heroic Bedell [47], but on the one hand of Chillingworth
and Hales; on the other of Ussher, Hall, and Dave-
nant: groups of names sharply severed in opinion, but
unitedly known in the history of ability and of learning.
It is directly to the present purpose to compare the
Calvinistic Oxford, to which Laud came as a youth,
with the Anglican Oxford which he quitted to pass out
into the government of affairs.

The change in this place almost recalls what was
said of Augustus, that he found Rome brick, and

---

[46] *History*, i. 86-9.
[47] Mant, *History of the Church of Ireland*, vol. i. p. 434.

left it marble; or, if the inverted form be preferred, Laud found Oxford marble, and left it brick: for it is the amount of the transformation, and not its quality, that I seek to indicate. This change was not wrought by a man having as yet the Star Chamber and High Commission at his back, but seemingly by his force of character and will. He went out into the world. He obtained hold of the helm. He gave to the Anglican polity and worship what was in the main the impress of his own mind. * He then sank to the ground in that conflict of the times, which he had much helped to exasperate. But his scheme of Church polity, for his it largely was, grew up afresh out of his tomb, and took effect in law at the Restoration. And now, with the mitigations which religious liberty has required, it still subsists in all its essential features, not as personal or party opinion, but as embodied alike in statute and in usage, with no apparent likelihood of disappearance or decay. Dealing still exclusively with the quantitative aspect of the case, and wholly apart from merits or demerits, I conceive that he, with Henry VIII and Queen Elizabeth, forms the triad of persons, who have had the largest share in giving to the momentous changes of the sixteenth century so much of their form as is strictly and specifically British. Such is an outline of the facts which have led me to appreciate so highly the brain-force of Laud.

So far, then, it would appear that the energies of Oxford have more largely taken effect than those of Cambridge in the world of action, as it is distinguished from the world of thought.

But we have been dealing with the ecclesiastical sphere alone. I incline to believe that in the province of lay life, once narrower but now wider by much, and ever widening more and more, we might arrive at the same comparative result. But the process of inquiry is far more arduous ; and the relation between the lay life of the country and the Universities is far more difficult to trace. Nor could it with advantage be brought down to the varied and multiplied developments of the present day.

Perhaps the department of political life, so far as it goes, would enable us better than most others to bring into juxtaposition the performances of our two ancient Universities. The contributions of Cambridge to the work of governing the country, during the last century, were large and brilliant. But I do not know whether she can allege any thing so telling in this respect as the following recital.

The usual practice of both has been to choose a Chancellor from an order not lower than that of Peers. In the year 1772 Oxford selected from among her *alumni*, to be her Chancellor, Frederic Lord North. From that day to this, from the election of Lord North to the election of Lord Salisbury, every one of her Chancellors, six in number, has also been, or has become, a Prime Minister of the country. The fact, taken in its rude outline, and without any attempt at the determination of relative rank between these and other statesmen, such as Pitt or Fox, Peel or Canning, seems to point to some specially strong tendency of Oxford methods towards the exigencies of public life.

I shall not, however, attempt to enter, even in the most general way, on the history or condition of Oxford or Cambridge during the nineteenth century. The enormous efforts which they have made for self-renovation and extension prove that, after so many ages, they still are young; and afford the brightest promise for their future. But it cannot be, as it was in the last century, a future of somnolent predominance. Youthful and active companions have come into the field, to extend the range of culture, and to insure its adaptation to modern wants: perhaps also to forbid relapses into lethargy, and to provide a fresh access of material for the finishing hand to work on. To secure their position, as well as to attain their proper ends, the nation will ask from her ancient and still paramount Universities a constant increase of energetic exertion. Doubtless they may learn one from the other; but neither, I trust, will ever be ashamed of its distinctive character, which has been maintained through the vicissitudes of so long a time. We have each, whether individuals or institutions, to recognise the determining lines of our own several formations, which are in truth conditions essential for turning those formations to the best account[48]. The chief dangers before them are probably two : one that in research, considered as apart from their teaching office, they should relax and consequently

---

[48] ' En toutes choses, l'individualité est une des premières conditions de succès : on ne fait bien que ce qu'on fait en demeurant soi-même.' Chastel, *Décadence du Paganisme dans l'Orient.*

dwindle; the other that, under pressure from without, they should lean, if ever so little, to that theory of education, which would have it to construct machines of so many horse-power, rather than to form character, and to rear into true excellence the marvellous creature we call man; which gloats upon success in life, instead of studying to secure that the man shall ever be greater than his work, and never bounded by it, but that his eye shall boldly run (in the language of Wordsworth)

Along the line of limitless desires.

And this leads us nearly back to the point from which we began. The University, at its inception, was at least in its secondary aspect a guarantee against the unchecked predominance of the ecclesiastical order. The spiritual and the temporal or secular elements, so to call them, dwelt side by side through a long course of generations, in standing competition, even in occasional strife, but in strife which never even threatened to become estrangement. They worked, upon the whole, in concert; and jointly they achieved a noble result. It is not among the favourable signs of our own era, that this concord has been broken, in some European countries, by the total expulsion or disappearance of theology from the academic precinct[49]. I have no fear of our witnessing here any

---

[49] The latest act in this retrograde operation has been, I fear, in Italy, which may be said to have given the Universities to Christendom. In every one of her Universities, as I understand, the theological faculty has been extinguished.

similar severance between the constituent parts of sound and thorough education. It may be that the circumstances, and some even of the measures of our time, have not been propitious to the cultivation of one great branch of human knowledge, and have borne the marks of an inevitable reaction from undue clerical preponderance. Such reactions are essentially temporary; and will not prevent theology from recovering whatever ground may be due to it in virtue of its own proper force. I speak of theology as a science; and not of this theology or that. And it seems no violent paradox to say that, if there be a Creator of this universe, the knowledge which reverently deals with our relations to Him can hardly be other than the crown of human knowledge. It can, then, hardly fail to offer the richest reward, as well as to advance the most commanding claim, to the service and devotion not of stunted or of crippled intellects, but of the very flower of our youth.

Whether, as some think, the idea of an University in its comprehensive fulness has always been, or has not, an essentially Christian conception, it cannot, I suppose, be open to an historic doubt that the central idea of our ancient English Universities is an idea essentially Christian [50]. It is nowhere more simply, and nowhere

---

[50] Cardinal Newman, in his work on the idea of an University, has set forth, with much of his own peculiar charm, the claims of Athens and Alexandria to have first embodied this great conception. He does not, however, convince me that either the one or the other in any way deprives Christendom of the honours of originality. Let us take the facts as he seems to present them.

more nobly, conveyed than in the motto of Oxford, *Dominus illuminatio mea*. May the day never come, when that ensign shall be changed, or when there shall be the smallest inkling of a desire to change it to its opposite, and to proclaim *Dominus obscuratio mea, Dominus obtenebratio mea*. May that root, and atmosphere, and light, which yield the best in leaf and flower and fruit, and which feed humanity up to its highest excellence for the performance of its great office in creation, be more and more, from age to age, the root, and the atmosphere, and the light, which shall sustain the life of Oxford in the generations yet to come!

Athens exhibits the action of schools which were voluntary and brilliant, with some degree of continuity or succession, but isolated, and in philosophy alone. Alexandria has much more of elaborate equipment and definite history, but presents a mechanism not merely aided but devised and ordered by the State, rather than an institution that worked by an independent life dwelling within itself.

NOTES

I. ON BISHOP BERKELEY

On reflection, I think that though much of Berkeley's heart was in Oxford, his residence was too short to allow of our claiming his name. On the other hand, I allow myself the pleasure of adding Chatham, who was a member of Trinity College, to the great names of Oxford in the last century.

II. ON BISHOP BUTLER

My statement, that no portion of Bishop Butler's works had ever been translated, was insufficiently considered and might have been corrected in part by reference to Brunet. A needful limitation was at once supplied by Dr. Emil Reich, who in a letter dated Oct. 25 gave the following valuable information.

There are two German and one French translation of Bishop Butler's immortal work, viz. :—

Jos. Buttler (*sic*).—*Bestätigung der natürlichen und geoffenbarten Religion*; aus dem Englischen, von J. J. Spalding. (Leipsic, 1756, 8vo. New edition, Tübingen, 1779.)

Jos. Buttler (*sic*).—*Uebereinstimmung der natürlichen und geoffenbarten Religion*, umgearbeitet...von C. H. Schreyer. (Leipsic,

1787.) See C. H. Kayser's *Vollständiges Bücherlexicon* (Leipsic, 1834), vol. i. p. 400. Compare O. Zoeckler, *Geschichte der Beziehungen zwischen Theologie und Naturwissenschaft* (Gütersloh, 1875), vol. ii. p. 251, note 42).

Jos. Butler.—*L'Analogie de la Religion naturelle et révélée, avec l'ordre et le cours de la nature, par J. B.* Traduit de l'anglais. (Paris, 1821.) See Brunet, *Table Méthodique*, No. 1,800.

On the 27th, Dr. Reich added a list of notices of Butler by German and French writers.

The following Continental works contain elaborate notices and appreciations of the Bishop's leading ideas :—

Schroeckh.—*Christliche Kirchengeschichte seit der Reformation* (Leipsic, 1804-1812), part vi. p. 231 *sq.*

Henke (H. Ph. C.).—*Allgemeine Geschichte der Christlichen Kirche* (Brunswick, 1818 *sq.*), part vi. p. 136.

Zoeckler (Otto).—*Theologia Naturalis* (in German). Frankfort-on-Main, 1860, pp. 100-102.

Zoeckler (Otto).—*Geschichte der Beziehungen zwischen Theologie und Naturwissenschaft* (Gütersloh, 1879), part ii. pp. 80-82.

Jouffroy (Th. S.).—*Cours de Droit naturel* (Paris, 1843), 19me leçon.

Carrau (L.).—*La Philosophie religieuse en Angleterre depuis Locke jusqu'à nos jours*, chapters ii and iii (Paris, 1888).

This list might have been enlarged by reference to Lotze and, I believe, to others.

But on the question of translations I have still to observe as follows.

1. It does not appear, thus far, that any work of Butler except the *Analogy*, and in particular that the *Sermons*, have ever been translated.

2. The only translation executed into any tongue except the German appears to have been that of 1821, in French. But my venerated friend, the Bishop of Bath and Wells,

has given me the history of this translation. It was not due to any French demand, but to his father, the Marquis of Bristol, who executed it with the aid of a French Abbé. He had many French friends, and wished to put it in their power to read a book which he himself so highly valued.

3. The only real exception, therefore, is in Germany, which, as usual in these matters, sets the good example. But even Germany has not required any translation except of the *Analogy*, or any fresh issue of that work for the last 105 years.

I have further learned with much interest—through the courtesy of the Rev. Mr. Shirreff—that some translations from Butler into Hindostanee have been executed in India, in connection with missionary purposes.

www.ingramcontent.com/pod-product-compliance
Lightning Source LLC
Chambersburg PA
CBHW021238260626
47172CB00002B/825